That night, as the boys slept . . .

. . . something strange crashed down at Commonwealth Elementary School.

10

13

21

29

31

ABOUT THE AUTHOR

Growing up, Scott Nickel wanted to be a comic book writer or a mad scientist. As an adult, he gets to do both. In his secret literary lab, Scott has created more than a dozen graphic novels for Stone Arch Books featuring time travelers, zombies, robots, giant insects, and mutant lunch ladies. Scott's *Night of the Homework Zombies* received the 2007 Golden Duck award for Best Science Fiction Picture Book. When not creating crazy comics, Scott squeezes in a full-time job as a writer and editor at Jim Davis's Garfield studio. He lives in Muncie, Indiana, with his wife, two teenage sons, and an ever-growing number of cats.

ABOUT THE ILLUSTRATOR

Matt Luxich started drawing at three years old. Although his parents didn't enjoy cleaning their son's cartoons off of the walls, they supported his talent. Years later, Luxich attended the Kubert School of Illustration and Animation in Dover, New Jersey. Today, he uses the skills he learned at school in his job as a freelance illustrator and designer, working for clients such as Golden Books and the Salvation Army. When he's not drawing, Luxich likes to eat cheese slices, play with toy robots, and walk his English Bulldog, Dover.

GLOSSARY

cafeteria (kaf-uh-TIHR-ee-uh)—a place where food is served at a counter and then taken to a table; a cafeteria is often called a lunchroom.

defeat (di-FEET)—to beat someone at a competition

encyclopedias (en-sye-kluh-PEE-dee-uhz)—those thick, dusty books in the library, which contain information on many different subjects

geography (jee-OG-ruh-fee)—the study of Earth, including its people, climate, and physical features

inhaler (in-HAY-lur)—a small device used to breathe in medicine through the mouth

permission (pur-MISH-uhn)—allowing someone to do something they ask to do

pioneer (pye-uh-NEER)—a person who explores new and unknown lands; the first settlers of the American West were pioneers.

zombie (ZOM-bee)—someone whose brain is controlled by another person; when you tell your friend to eat worms, and he does it, he is acting like a zombie.

MORE ABOUT ALIENS AND UFOS

Could aliens really come to Earth and turn your teachers into homework-crazed creatures? Maybe they already have! Well, maybe not. But many people believe aliens have visited Earth thousands of times.

Every year, people around the world report seeing unidentified flying objects, also known as UFOs. Although most people see UFOs in the sky at night, their sizes and shapes often vary. Some report flying saucers or large objects shaped like triangles. Others have seen flashing lights, which are too bright to be airplanes.

Some believe UFO sightings have only happened recently. But in fact, people have believed in alien visitors for thousands of years. Ancient Mayans lived in Central America nearly 3,500 years ago. These people believed their gods came from the stars.

Many ancient artifacts and monuments are linked to aliens. The Great Pyramids in Egypt and Stonehenge in Britain are two of the most famous. Some believe humans could not have lifted the gigantic stones used to build these monuments. Instead, they claim creatures from another planet constructed the sites.

Perhaps the most famous alien sighting happened in Roswell, New Mexico, on June 14, 1947. That night, people reported seeing several "flying discs" in the sky. At a local ranch, farmer William "Mac" Brazel discovered the wreckage of a strange aircraft. The U.S. Army quickly cleaned up the debris, saying it was nothing more than a simple weather balloon. Many believe the Army found an alien spaceship and has tried to cover it up ever since.

After the sighting in Roswell, New Mexico, President Harry S. Truman created a top-secret group to investigate aliens and UFOs. This group is often known as the Majestic 12. Of course, since the group was top secret, the U.S. government denies that it ever existed.

So, have UFOs visited Earth? From 1947 to 1970, the U.S. Air Force investigated 12,618 UFO sightings in a program called Project Blue Book. When they had finished, the officials concluded that many of the sightings were hoaxes or simply stars in the sky. But even their scientists could not explain 701 of the reports. The question remains a mystery.

DISCUSSION QUESTIONS

1. How did Trevor's relationship with Filbert change throughout the book? Do you think Trevor liked Filbert at the beginning of the story? Do you think Trevor liked Filbert at the end of the story? Explain your answers using examples from the book.

2. On page 15, Trevor lied to get permission to leave the classroom. If he hadn't lied, the aliens might have taken over the school. Do you think he should still be punished for lying to his teacher? Explain.

3. This book was written and illustrated by two different people. If you had a choice, would you rather be an author or an illustrator? Explain your decision.

WRITING PROMPTS

1. Write your own alien adventure. What do your aliens look like? Are they good or evil? Describe how you would greet the aliens when they first arrive on Earth.

2. Pretend you are the author and write another tale about Trevor versus the zombies. Where will the zombies show up this time? The choice is up to you.

3. In this story, we learn that Trevor's friend, Filbert, loves school and encyclopedias. But we don't learn much else about him. Write your own story about Filbert's family, friends, pets, and hobbies.

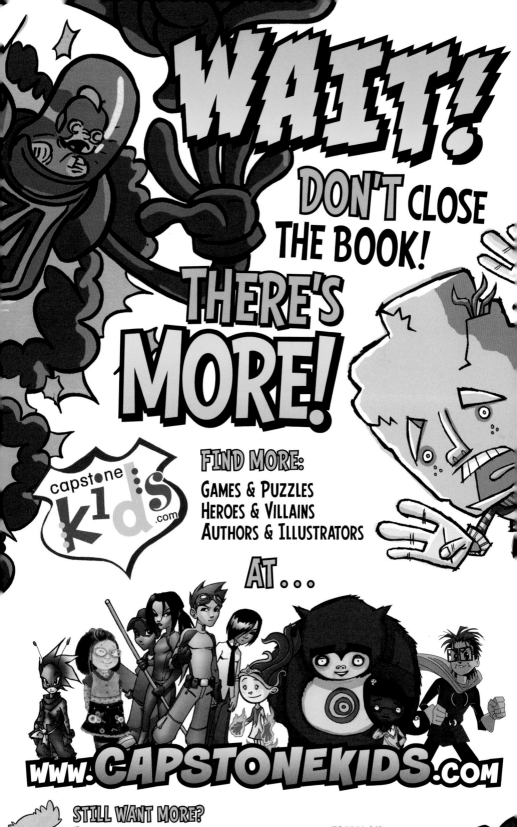

Graphic Sparks are published by Stone Arch Books,
A Capstone Imprint
1710 Roe Crest Drive
North Mankato, Minnesota 56003
www.capstonepub.com

Library of Congress Cataloging-in-Publication Data
Nickel, Scott.
    Secret of the Summer School Zombies / by Scott Nickel; illustrated by Matt Luxich.
    p. cm. — (Graphic Sparks. School Zombies)
    ISBN 978-1-4342-0760-9 (library binding)
    ISBN 978-1-4342-0856-9 (pbk.)
    1. Graphic novels. [1. Graphic novels. 2. Schools—Fiction. 3. Zombies—Fiction.]
I. Luxich, Matt, ill. II. Title.
PZ7.7.N53Se 2009
[Fic]—dc22   2008006710

Summary: Trevor thought nothing could be worse than spending the entire summer in
school. Then his teachers turn into homework-crazed creatures! Now Trevor and his friend
Filbert must find a way to stop the zombies. Or they'll be trapped inside the classroom of
doom forever!

Art Director: Heather Kindseth
Graphic Designer: Brann Garvey

Printed in the United States of America.
012017
10233R

SECRET

SUMMER SCHOOL ZOMBIES

Librarian Reviewer
Katharine Kan
Graphic novel reviewer and Library Consultant, Panama City, FL
MLS in Library and Information Studies, University of Hawaii at
Manoa, HI

Reading Consultant
Elizabeth Stedem
Educator/Consultant, Colorado Springs, CO
MA in Elementary Education, University of Denver, CO

STONE ARCH BOOKS
www.stonearchbooks.com